Knights' Tales

The Knight of

vords and Spooks

Bloomsbury Education
An imprint of Bloomsbury Publishing Plc

50 Bedford Square	1385 Broadway
London	New York
WC1B 3DP	NY 10018
UK	USA

www.bloomsbury.com

BLOOMSBURY and the Diana logo are trademarks of Bloomsbury Publishing Plc

First published in 2009 by A & C Black , an imprint of Bloomsbury Publishing Plc
This paperback edition published in 2018

A catalogue record for this book is available from the British Library.

ISBN

PB: 978 1 4729 4206 7
epub: 978 1 4729 5305 6
epdf: 978 1 4729 5306 3

2 4 6 8 10 9 7 5 3 1

Printed and bound in UK by CPI Group (UK) ltd, Croydon CR0 4YY

To find out more about our authors and books visit www.bloomsbury.com. Here you will find extracts,
author interviews, details of forthcoming events and the option to sign up for our newsletters.

TERRY DEARY

Knights' Tales

The Knight of Swords and Spooks

Inside illustrations by Helen Flook

BLOOMSBURY EDUCATION
AN IMPRINT OF BLOOMSBURY

LONDON OXFORD NEW YORK NEW DELHI SYDNEY

CHAPTER ONE
Boy and Boar

England, 1485

Sir Thomas Stanley sat at the window and enjoyed the late-summer sun. It shone

through the diamond panes of glass and onto his velvet jacket the colour of rust. He chewed on a peach and looked out over the fine garden of his castle.

There was a soft knock at the door and Sir Thomas called, "Enter!"

A boy pushed open the door – a fair-haired, pale boy in a green tunic. He was carrying a wooden sword.

"Ah, George, my son! Come in, come in!" Sir Thomas said, waving a hand.

The boy stood in front of his father's chair. "You sent for me, Father?"

"I did, George, I did!" The man smiled. It was a wide smile and as honest as a snake that is just about to swallow a rabbit.

"I was practising my riding with a lance. Robin was teaching me."

"Good boy, good boy. We need all the knights we can get to fight our wars. There will always be wars and there will always be knights! Ha! Now, my dear, dear son..."

George blinked. His father had never called him 'dear' before. In fact, he thought his father hardly knew he was alive and living in the same castle. At dinner, his father sat with his favourite knights and ladies at the top table. George sat with the children and the squires.

"As you know," Sir Thomas was saying, "when a boy reaches your age, he is sent away to live with another family. It's a chance for a lad to see how other great families do things... get to see other parts of England... meet new people."

"Yes, Father."

"Now, I have the most thrilling news. It is so exciting I can hardly believe it myself, my dear, dear son."

"You are sending me away to serve as a squire to a knight."

"Not just *any* knight."

"A great knight?"

"Not just *any* great knight!" Sir Thomas Stanley chuckled. "You, my dear son, are going to serve in the palace of the king himself!"

"The king?" George said. "Why?"

"Why? Why what?"

"Why me? The king has thousands of fine families to choose from. Why me?"

Sir Thomas shifted in his seat as if it were hot. "Don't ask questions like that, boy. Now... turn around and kneel before King Richard III!"

George turned slowly. Sitting in a darkened corner of the room was a man with skin as pale as plaster. Dark eyes burned in a sad face with thin lips. The man was dressed in black. It was plain, black wool, not the fine silk George would expect from a king. Only a badge in the shape of a white boar on his riding cloak and a large golden ring on his finger gave some colour.

The king sat hunched in the chair and stared at George in a way that made the boy shiver.

A tall man was standing behind the chair. He smiled a sneering smile. George fell to one knee and bowed before the king.

King Richard spoke in a harsh voice. "Sir Richard Ratcliffe here will be your keeper," he said.

The king stood up. He was not a tall man and he walked with a limp. He passed the kneeling boy and went to stand beside

Sir Thomas. "He will do," he said.

Sir Thomas wrung his hands. "Oh, thank you, Sire."

"Do not let me down, Thomas Stanley, or you know what will happen," he said quietly, and his voice was hard as frost.

Sir Thomas smiled a frightened smile and bowed low. Then the king was gone.

Ratcliffe slapped the boy on his back. "Get your servant – what's his name? Robin? Get him to pack your saddlebags. We ride for Nottingham Castle as soon as you are ready."

George hurried to the door.

"Goodbye, George," Sir Thomas said. There was something in the way he said it that made George think he meant 'Goodbye... forever'.

CHAPTER TWO
Tudor and Traitor

Robin groaned as he packed George Stanley's saddlebags. Then he spoke a curious rhyme:

> *"The Rat, the Cat, and Lovell the Dog,*
> *Rule all England under the Hog."*

"What does that mean?" George asked.

Robin shook his head. He was an old man, wise in the ways of teaching a knight, but feeble in body now. "I shouldn't have said that! But... but the Rat is the man you've just met... Sir Richard Ratcliffe – one of King Richard's most trusted knights. The Cat is another... Sir William Catesby. And Lovell is Lord Francis Lovell... the king's favourite."

"They rule England?"

"With the help of the Hog – that's King Richard himself," Robin whispered.

"You can't call the king a hog!" George whispered back.

"It's his badge – a wild boar – a hog," Robin explained.

"Robin?"

"Yes, Master George."

"Why are we whispering?"

"Ah... the man who made up that rhyme about the Rat, the Cat, and Lovell the Dog was called Collingham. When the king heard about it, he had Collingham executed. So never call Ratcliffe the Rat!"

The old servant gripped the boy by the shoulders. "You are heading into terrible danger, Master George."

George shook his head.

"I'm going to train to be a knight. I may be knocked off my horse once or twice, but it's not real danger!" he smiled.

Robin did not return the smile. "Is that what your father told you?" he asked.

"Yes," George said. "Why? Would Father lie to me? What is the truth?"

The door to George's room was open and Ratcliffe stood there with his sour mouth turned down at the corners. "Truth about what?"

George had learned Robin's lessons well – a knight does not show fear. "What is the truth about my journey to Nottingham?"

Ratcliffe glared at the boy. "England is in terrible danger," he said, and he sat on a stool by the door. He took out his dagger and used the point to clean his nails as he talked.

"*Danger*?" George asked.

"There is an enemy of the king called Henry Tudor – he has landed in Wales and he is gathering an army. He wants to take the throne from King Richard."

The boy gasped. "And the king wants *me* to fight?"

Ratcliffe sneered. "No, the king wants your *father* to fight. Your father and your uncle Will can command five or six thousand men. The king needs those men in his army. There is a great battle coming. One of the greatest England has ever seen. King Richard has to win it."

"He'll win with my father's help," George

said. He had seen the soldiers in the fields outside the castle, and watched them train, with the archers sending so many arrows into the sky that the sun turned dark.

Knights practised their fighting on horseback and on foot – swinging swords

and axes and heavy clubs they called maces. They rode back into the castle each night to rest and seemed happy. The Stanley army was ready to fight.

Sir Richard Ratcliffe stood up and placed the knife point under the boy's chin. "Yes, young George. With your father's help we *will* win... but what if your father does *not* help?"

"Not help?"

"What if your father turned traitor and fought for Henry Tudor? Then we would lose. You see the problem?"

"Why would my father fight for Henry Tudor?"

Ratcliffe nodded. "I suppose they don't tell you things like that. Henry Tudor is your father's stepson... *your* stepbrother. Sir Thomas may switch sides and fight for Henry. So, we need a *hostage*." The knife tip pricked the soft skin of George's throat.

"And if your father betrays King Richard... then you know what will happen?"

Suddenly George *did* know. "You will kill me?"

This time, Ratcliffe gave a real, wide smile. "Oh, yes, little George. We will kill you!"

CHAPTER THREE
Cheers and Chains

The ride to Nottingham was grim. George was always watched by three men-at-arms. His servant Robin was forced to ride at the back with the baggage wagon and Sir Richard Ratcliffe hardly spoke.

Nottingham Castle loomed above them and even on that summer day it seemed cold and unfriendly.

The fields outside the town were littered with tents of all sorts. Some were fine ones with coloured stripes for the lords, and some were ragged shelters for the poorest archers and foot soldiers.

Cooking fires covered the fields with a haze of smoke, but through the smoke George could still smell the foul scent of the toilet pits and the filthy men.

From time to time, he saw knights practising with lances, while soldiers watched and cheered from the banks.

The gates in the city walls were crammed with people hurrying in and out, carts carrying food and weapons, beggars trying to cadge coppers and teams of huge horses pulling mighty bronze cannon along the roads.

Ratcliffe's small troop waited for the traffic at the gate to clear, and that allowed Robin to catch up with George on his pony.

"Look at the crowds!" Robin said cheerfully. "If you slip away, they'll never find you in this mob!"

"Slip away?"

"Escape! Save your life, Master George. The first chance we get, we'll flee. My family in Lancashire will look after you until this is over... even if Henry Tudor wins, your father will be safe."

"So I will be safe?"

"No, no!" Robin moaned. "If your father helps Henry Tudor to win, then you will be too dead to enjoy the victory – Ratcliffe will see to that!"

The men-at-arms pushed George ahead and through a gap in the crowd. Inside the city walls, the market stalls were in danger of being crushed by the masses and even the houses were shaking. Only the mighty castle looked safe and solid. But, once he was inside, George knew he would never escape.

As they came near the gatehouse, he looked around. His guards were talking to the soldiers at the gate. Robin sat at the back of the line and nodded his head. The old man climbed down from his pony, stiff and aching from the ride.

George took one last look and tumbled down from his saddle; as soon as his boots touched the cobbles, he was running back down the road.

Robin swept a cloak over the boy's head and dragged him down an alley and into a doorway.

They were lost before Ratcliffe knew they were gone. The doorway led into a tavern. The tavern was jammed with men looking for ale to wash away the dust of the scorching day. There was no way to fight their way through the crowd.

Robin saw a gap between two women and slipped into it, but the gap closed before George could follow. He was stuck at the doorway.

There were angry voices in the alley and a young woman cried, "They went that way, My Lord... into the tavern..." and then, "Ohhh! Thank you, Sire," as Sir Richard Ratcliffe handed her a piece of silver from his purse.

Soon Ratcliffe's sunburned face loomed over George and his strong hand grasped the boy's hood and dragged him from the doorway.

"I should kill you for this, you little puppy. And when the battle is over I *will* kill you. No matter what happens, I *will* kill you!" he snarled. "For now, I need you alive... but your old servant will die in the castle dungeons as soon as we find him."

Robin, however, was nowhere to be seen.

"A knight – a true knight – would not try to escape from a promise his father made. From now on," Ratcliffe said, "you will not be treated like a young knight. You will be treated like the miserable prisoner you are. From now on, you will be held in chains – chains as hard as King Richard's heart."

CHAPTER FOUR
Tower and Torment

The army marched from Nottingham two days later. It stretched for miles along the English roads.

At its head was the round-shouldered shape of King Richard III. And, just behind him, his prisoner, chained to a pony and guarded by the menacing Ratcliffe.

The king led his army westwards to where he knew the enemy was coming. "You will see how a knight fights," Richard promised the boy. "What is your name, young Stanley?"

"George, Your Majesty."

"Ha! George, eh? I had a brother called George, you know?"

"No, Sire."

"Yes, *Brother* George," he said bitterly.

"What happened to him?" the boy asked.

"He betrayed us. Took sides with our enemies... I had to have him executed in the Tower of London. My own brother. You cannot trust anyone. And I do not trust your father."

"He's still my father," George said. "I cannot call him a traitor."

King Richard nodded. "You are a good knight – and a loyal son. I had a son, you know."

"I didn't know."

"He died. A baby. Children die. You shall die if your father betrays me. Are you afraid?"

"No, Sire."

Richard laughed and rode on.

That night, they reached a field that the soldiers called Bosworth. They set up their camp in the warm evening air.

To the south and the west, the hills were gentle and green. In the distance, the sky was clouded orange.

Ratcliffe looked out of the tent where George was chained to the main pole. "Only an army makes a dust cloud like that. Henry Tudor is on his way. Tomorrow there'll be a battle."

"What will happen? George asked.

"We will win," the tall knight answered. "You see, we are on a hilltop. Henry Tudor's men will have to march *up* the hill to attack. We will mow them down with our arrows, and they will be climbing over the corpses of their friends. If any of them *do* reach us, they will be too exhausted to fight our knights. We sit here. We wait. We win." The man raised an arm and pointed to the north. "See that hill a mile away?"

"Yes, My Lord."

"That's a place called Coton. Your father and your uncle are marching their army there now. When Henry Tudor attacks us, your Stanley armies will smash them from the side. We cannot lose."

George nodded. He lay back on a blanket. After a long day's ride he soon fell asleep. Deeply asleep. Yet he awoke in terror.

Hours had passed. It was darkest night. He wondered what had woken him. Then he heard it again. The screams of a man – a man in torment. He knew it came from the next tent.

Sir Richard Ratcliffe stumbled in the dark of their tent and threw on a cloak. He came back moments later with his arm around a shadowy figure. "It was a dream, just a dream," he murmured to the man.

The shadow-man gave a long groan. "It's a sign, Ratcliffe, a sign. A bad sign. Tomorrow... tomorrow in the battle... tomorrow, I will die!"

And the boy knew the tormented voice was the voice of King Richard.

CHAPTER FIVE
Night and Noon

King Richard sat on the floor of the tent and took deep breaths as if he were in pain. "Oh, Ratcliffe, the things I saw!"

"It was a dream, Your Majesty."

"Maybe, Ratcliffe... or maybe the gates of Hell opened up. The devil let out the spirits of the men and children I've murdered."

"You don't believe in spooks, Your Majesty," Ratcliffe said in a soothing voice.

"Remember Lord Hastings? He was my loyal friend. One night at dinner, I had him dragged outside and said I wouldn't eat until his head was cut off. The  guards found a plank of wood and used that instead of a block. A sword instead of an axe. I saw him last night, Ratcliffe! He came back to haunt me!"

"Hush, Your Majesty. The men will take it as a bad sign. They will be afraid before they go into battle."

But the king wasn't listening. "The princes... my nephews... my brother's boys. Locked in the Tower. Smothered to  death and buried in a secret grave."

"No, they were sickly children. They would have died anyway," Ratcliffe argued quietly.

"They died without a funeral – that means their spirits can't rest. I saw them, too, last night, Ratcliffe."

"A dream, Your Majesty."

"Ghosts, Ratcliffe. And I saw Lord Rivers... and... ohhhh! My brother George! Did I tell you about George?"

"The traitor?"

"He asked us not to behead him. He said if we *had* to execute him, we should drown him in a barrel of wine!" the king sobbed.

"Poor George. I saw him, too – he came to my tent. It is a sign, Ratcliffe, a sign."

The king moaned again and sank back onto the ground. In the darkness, young George heard him breathing heavily.

The boy fell into a restless sleep, too.

The noise of the camp, stirring at first light, woke him. King Richard sat up and looked across in his direction. The king's

face was as grey as any ghost. He turned
to Ratcliffe. "The boy?" he said. "The boy
heard what I said last night."

Ratcliffe gave a single nod.

The king rose to his feet. "We can't have
him telling the world that Richard is a
coward – spooked by dreams like a child,"
he hissed. "If the battle goes against us, he

has to die. Make sure it is done."

The two men turned towards the boy, their faces as twisted and ugly as ancient trees.

George looked back steadily.

A hooded man set George free from his chains. The battle had been thundering in the valley below, and George had been forgotten.

The hooded man also wore a mask that covered his face. He opened the lock and led George to the door of the tent. They looked down into the valley.

"What's happening?" George asked, anxiously.

The man spoke in a voice muffled by the mask. "Richard's first line charged down the hill at Henry Tudor," the guard said, and pointed to the valley to the west.

"Lord Ratcliffe said they'd wait here!" George argued. "He said it would be a mistake to charge off the hilltop!"

"A mistake," the man nodded. "It was. But it seemed the king didn't care to be careful. It seemed as if he was ready to die. He rode down at the head of the second charge... See? There he is!"

George could make out the round-shouldered knight in fine armour leading a charge of knights in the noonday sun.

They rippled like a silver stream in the light. But the army at the bottom was ready for them – a green flag with a red dragon waved over Henry Tudor.

The king's knights struggled to reach it, to smash the invader. But the dragon's soldiers chopped them down and swallowed them up.

On Coton Hill another army, the Stanley army, sat and watched. As the king's men died, Sir Thomas Stanley did nothing to help. George would die for that treachery, he knew.

At last, King Richard's horse was brought down, and soldiers with axes and swords swarmed around him like maggots over a piece of meat.

CHAPTER SIX
Helmet and Hood

"To the rescue!" Sir Richard Ratcliffe cried, as he gathered a fresh troop of knights. It was too late to rescue the king. All they could do was rescue his body.

A great cheer from the valley showed the Tudor army was winning.

Sir Richard Ratcliffe rode up to where George and the guard stood. As he turned to make his charge down the hill, he looked back. "Execute him!" he shouted at the man in the mask. "Kill the traitor's son!"

George gave a tiny smile. Of course – the

man in the mask wasn't just an *ordinary* guard. He was an *executioner* – men only wore masks if they had to execute their victims.

Ratcliffe slammed down the face-guard on his helmet. He lowered his lance and rode down the hill to join his king.

George turned to the man in the mask, who carried no axe – no weapon of any sort.

"My father *knew* I'd die," the boy said, "yet he did nothing to help."

The executioner shrugged. "Your father said he has other sons. If you die, he will not be broken-hearted."

George nodded. "Thank you, Father!" he shouted across the valley to the army that sat under the Stanley banner of yellow and green. The army that didn't lift a finger to save its king.

"Your father will be all right," the masked man said. "Henry Tudor is his stepson. The Stanley family will be rewarded well for what they did today."

"And my reward? The axe? Or the sword? Or will you smother me like the princes in the Tower? Or drown me in a barrel of wine like the other George? You have no weapon. How will you kill me?"

The executioner raised a withered hand to the top of his head... and pushed back the hood. Then he grasped the leather mask and tugged at it. "You have no idea how hot it's been inside this hood," he groaned. He gave a last pull and threw the mask away.

George stepped back and leaned against the tent pole.

The executioner grinned at him. "You don't really want me to kill you, do you?"

George looked at the old man – Robin, his servant. "No, Robin, I think I'd rather live."

The old servant wrapped the boy in a tight hug and the two laughed until they had no breath left.

The king's defeated soldiers were struggling back up the hill, running past the boy and his servant. Away from the terror of the Tudor invaders.

Robin turned north and led George towards the Stanley army and his father. A treacherous army. A silent army. Silent as the grave.

EPILOGUE

Richard III became King of England in 1483. Some say he murdered his nephews, aged twelve and nine, to make sure he got it: they were imprisoned in the Tower of London and never seen again.

Richard had been on the throne only two years when Henry Tudor invaded. Richard's last stand was at Bosworth. With the help of the Stanley army, he should have crushed the invader. To make sure of them, Richard held Lord Stanley's son George hostage. George did try to escape, but was caught.

Richard had no pity for children – but, the night before the battle, it is said he suffered terrible nightmares. Maybe he really was haunted by the thoughts of the people he had killed.

At the last great battle, Richard charged down the hill with his knights – and this was the last great charge of armoured knights in British history... maybe even in world history. The Stanley family betrayed the king, and Richard died fighting as a knight.

There would be no more battles like that. The world of the knight was over forever. Even the bravest knight was no use against the cannon that armies started to use.

Henry Tudor became King Henry VII, the first of the ruthless Tudor kings and queens. If Henry had lost the battle, his son, the famous Henry VIII, or granddaughter, Elizabeth I, would never have been rulers of England. History changed on that one day, the 22nd of August 1485.

The Stanley family was safe when Henry won the battle – but the Rat, the Cat, and Lovell the Dog were not. Ratcliffe died in the battle, and Catesby was executed three days afterwards. Lovell's skeleton was found in a dungeon a year later – it seems he had starved to death.

It was fine and glorious to be a knight... but only when you were on the winning side.

YOU TRY

1. Tower Terror

Richard III imprisoned his nephews, Prince Edward and Prince Richard, when they were twelve and nine years old. He put them in the Tower of London – but the Tower was a castle in those days, not just a prison, and the boys didn't spend their days under lock and key.

They played at archery in the gardens inside the walls, but could never see their mother. The food would have been good and the servants kind, but nights would have been cold and damp.

Imagine you are Prince Edward. Write a letter to your mother telling her about life in the Tower for you and Richard. Remember, you don't know your fate – so you could also tell her what you plan to do when Uncle Richard says it is safe for you to leave the Tower and be crowned King Edward V.

2. Fine Feasting

If you'd like to taste some of the food that may have cheered up the princes in the Tower, ask an adult to help you try this tasty treat that rich people ate in the days of Richard III.

Eggs in Moonlight

You need: 100 ml water, 60 ml rose water, 75 g caster sugar, 3 eggs and some muffins or toast.

Heat the water, rose water and sugar in a small frying pan until the sugar dissolves and the water boils.

Crack in the eggs, one by one, and boil until the whites are cooked but the yolks are still soft.

Serve the eggs on warm, buttered toast or muffins, and pour over some of the rose water and sugar juice.